BILLY AND BLAZE

BILLY AND BLAZE

BY C. W. ANDERSON

Aladdin Paperbacks

Revised Cover Edition, 2000
Aladdin Paperbacks
An imprint of Simon & Schuster
Children's Publishing Division
1230 Avenue of the Americas
New York, NY 10020
Copyright © 1936 by Macmillan Publishing Co., Inc.
Copyright renewed 1964 by C. W. Anderson
First paperback edition, 1971
First Aladdin Paperbacks edition, 1992

Printed in China

28 30 29 27

Library of Congress Cataloging-in-Publication Data

Anderson, C. W. (Clarence William), 1891–1971.
Billy and Blaze : a boy and his pony / C. W. Anderson.
p.   cm. —(The Billy and Blaze books)
Summary: A little boy who loves horses gets a special birthday present.
ISBN 978-0-689-71608-9
[1. Horses—Fiction.]   I. Title.   II. Series: Anderson, C. W. (Clarence William), 1891–1971.   Billy
and Blaze books.
PZ7.A524Bi   1992
[E]—dc20   91-29882
0512 SCP

To Bob

Billy was a little boy who loved horses more than anything else in the world.

Whenever he had a chance to ride some farmer's horse, he used to pretend that it was a prancing pony.

One birthday morning his father said to him, "Out on the lawn you will find your birthday present."

And there stood a beautiful bay pony
with four white feet and a white nose.
Billy had never been so happy.

No boy was ever more proud and happy
than Billy when he went out for his
first ride. Right from the very start Billy
and his new pony seemed to like and
understand each other.

After thinking for a long time about many names, Billy decided to call the pony Blaze because he had a white blaze down his face.

Before going to bed that first night he took a flashlight and went down to the stable to see if Blaze was all right. Already Blaze seemed to feel at home and he was glad to see him.

As soon as it was daylight, Billy was up
cleaning and brushing Blaze so they
could take a long ride after breakfast.

It was not long before Blaze would come galloping whenever Billy called, for he knew there would be a carrot or a piece of sugar for him as well as much petting. And he, too, enjoyed the rides through the woods where there was so much to see.

One day, when they were riding along a path through the woods, they came to a tree fallen across the path and Blaze jumped quickly over it. Billy was so surprised he almost fell off. But it was very exciting and he decided to try it again.

So when they came to the next small
fence he leaned forward and gripped
with his knees and over they sailed.
It felt like flying.

One day in the woods they heard a dog howling as if in pain. They rode to the spot, and there they found a dog caught in a trap that had probably been set for some wild animals.

Although the dog was badly hurt, he seemed to know that Billy was trying to help him. He stood very still while Billy opened the trap and set him free. And then he limped along home with Billy and Blaze.

When they got home Billy bandaged the dog's foot and gave him something to eat. He was very hungry.

The dog seemed to have no home. No one could find out where he came from, so Billy's father let him keep him. He named the dog Rex, and, wherever Billy went, there you were sure to find Rex too.

Rex and Blaze were great friends. He
went down to the stable to see Blaze
very often and usually slept there with
him.

One day when Billy and Blaze were out riding they saw a sign on a tree telling about a horse show and a silver cup that was to be given to the best pony. "Let's try for it," said Billy to Blaze.

When Billy got to the show with Blaze and Rex and saw how many fine ponies were there, he began to be afraid that he might not win the cup after all.

But one pony after another knocked
down the rail when he jumped, and
Billy began to feel that Blaze might win
after all. He knew that he and Blaze
had often jumped over fences almost as
high as these.

At last Billy's turn came. Blaze jumped
perfectly and Rex jumped beside him.
Everybody clapped and cheered. Rex was
not supposed to jump, but everybody
liked to see a dog jump so well.

"You have a fine pony," said the judge as he gave Billy a silver cup almost too big for him to hold. A man came out and took a picture of all three of them. Then the judge pinned a blue ribbon on Blaze's bridle, with FIRST PRIZE printed in gold letters on it.

The grass and trees looked very green and the birds sang very gaily as the three went home. Blaze seemed to know he had done well, for he carried his head very high and pranced all the way.

Billy was as happy as any boy could be. For Blaze's supper that evening he brought many carrots and much sugar, and Rex had the finest bone in the house.

Billy set the silver cup in his room.
Every time he looked at it, he was very,
very proud of Blaze. His pony was his
best friend.